FROZEN

AUTUMN
PUBLISHING

Published in 2024
First published in the UK by Autumn Publishing
An imprint of Igloo Books Ltd
Cottage Farm, NN6 0BJ, UK
Owned by Bonnier Books
Sveavägen 56, Stockholm, Sweden
www.igloobooks.com

0424 001
2 4 6 8 10 9 7 5 3 1
ISBN 978-1-83795-921-1

Cover designed by Stephen Jorgensen

Printed and manufactured in China

This book belongs to:

_____

Disney
FROZEN

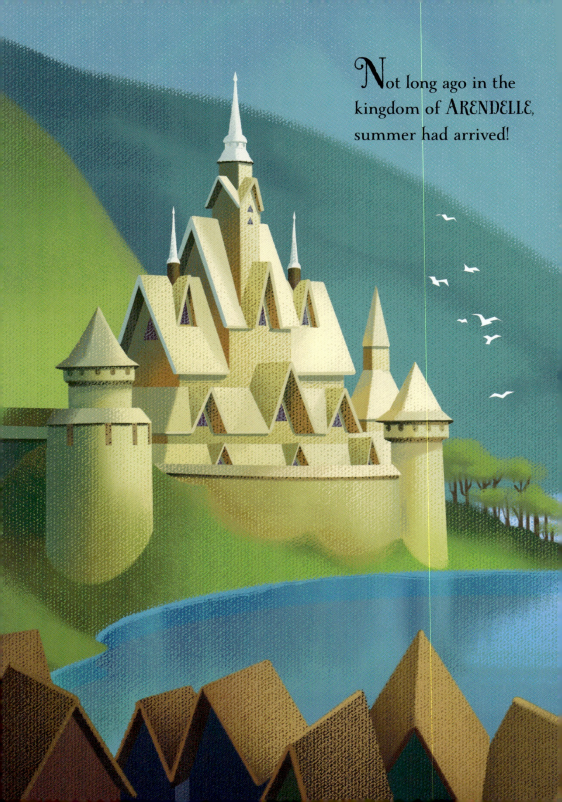

Not long ago in the kingdom of ARENDELLE, summer had arrived!

But it was winter inside the castle where
Princesses ELSA and ANNA were playing.
Elsa had magical powers and could create
things out of snow and ice! She made a
snowman named Olaf.
Anna was delighted.

Then Elsa accidentally hurt Anna.

The king and queen rushed both girls to
the mystical trolls in the mountains.

The trolls cured Anna by **CHANGING HER MEMORIES** of Elsa's magic. They cautioned that others would fear Elsa's power. To help her control it, Elsa's parents gave her gloves.

With the castle gates closed, Elsa stayed away from Anna – she never wanted to hurt her again.

But Elsa missed
ANNA.

Anna
missed
ELSA

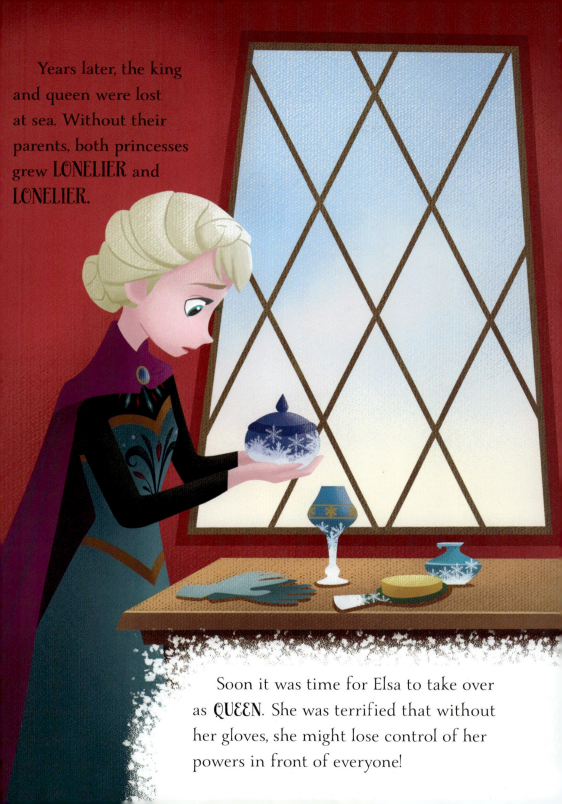

Years later, the king and queen were lost at sea. Without their parents, both princesses grew LONELIER and LONELIER.

Soon it was time for Elsa to take over as QUEEN. She was terrified that without her gloves, she might lose control of her powers in front of everyone!

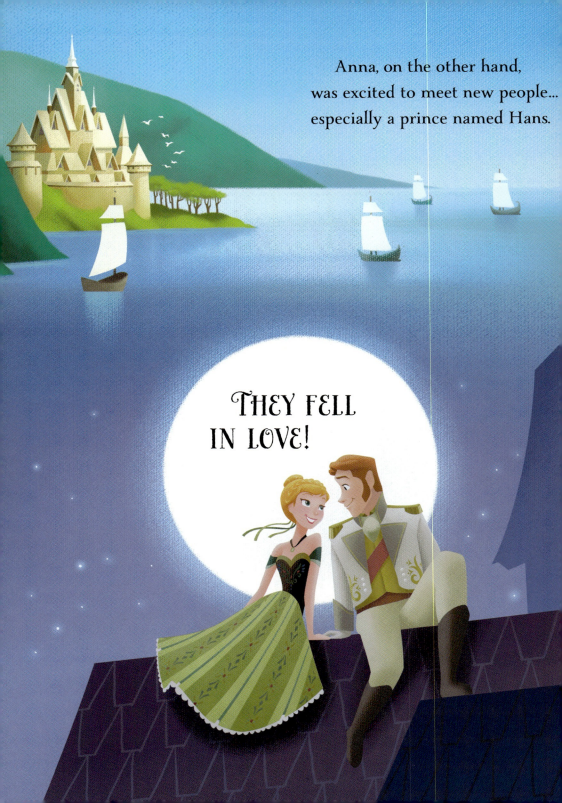

Anna, on the other hand,
was excited to meet new people...
especially a prince named Hans.

THEY FELL
IN LOVE!

Elsa gathered all her courage to take off her gloves,
and was successfully crowned Queen of Arendelle!

With her gloves back on, Elsa proudly stood before her people.

But when Anna told Elsa that she wanted to marry Hans, Elsa forbade it. How could Anna want to marry a man she had only just met?

Frustrated, Anna tried to stop her sister and accidentally **PULLED OFF** one glove.

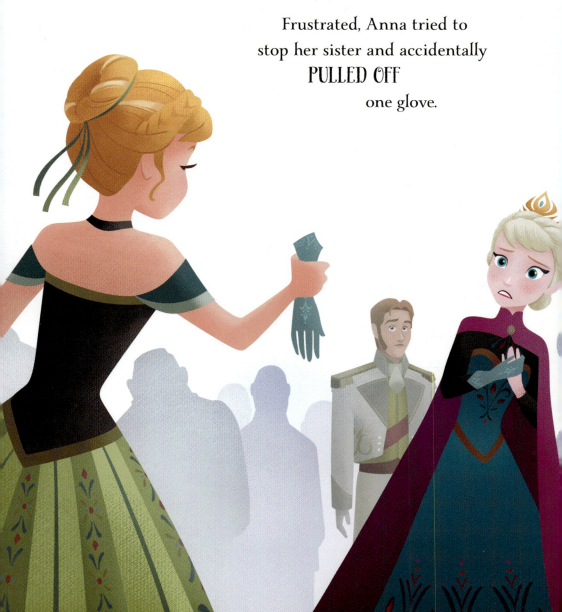

Without her glove and upset with Anna, Elsa accidentally exposed her secret powers. Ice and snow blasted from her hand, covering the kingdom.

Fearing she might hurt someone and ruin her kingdom, ELSA FLED.

Anna thought it was her fault Elsa's powers had been revealed. She rushed off to find her sister.

She hired a mountain man named Kristoff to be her guide.

In time, Anna and Kristoff found a snowman
named Olaf. He was alive!

Anna **REMEMBERED** him – and the good times she had
shared with her sister. Olaf led the way to Elsa.

Elsa was enjoying her time alone.

Now she was free to create whatever she wanted.

She built an ICE PALACE.

Anna begged Elsa to go home to thaw her frozen kingdom.
But Elsa feared she couldn't control her powers.

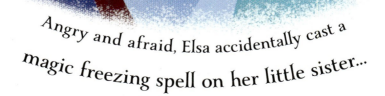

Angry and afraid, Elsa accidentally cast a magic freezing spell on her little sister...

... and then created a GIANT SNOWMAN.
Anna and Kristoff ran. Olaf ran, too!

Anna's hair began to turn white.
Kristoff led her to the trolls for help.

The trolls advised, "Only an
act of TRUE LOVE can thaw a
frozen heart."

Anna needed Hans
for a true love's kiss!

Quickly, Kristoff
and Anna headed
back to Arendelle.

When Anna found Hans, he REFUSED to iss her. His plan all along had been to take ver the kingdom. Anna was crushed!

Anna realised that Kristoff loved her!
She needed all her strength to find him.

Meanwhile, Elsa had returned to Arendelle to save her kingdom. But now she was in TERRIBLE DANGER.

When Anna saw Hans, she knew what she had to do.

Anna
SAVED
Elsa.

It was an act of true love – true love
BETWEEN TWO SISTERS.

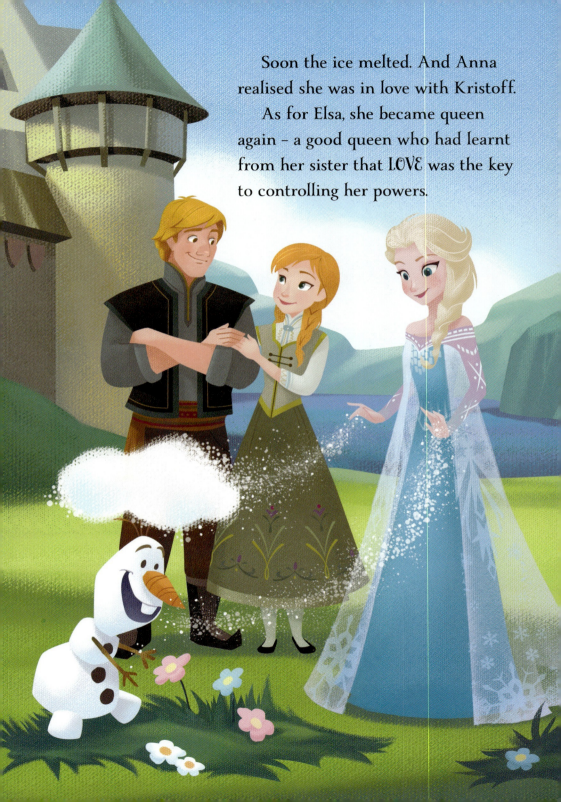

Soon the ice melted. And Anna realised she was in love with Kristoff. As for Elsa, she became queen again – a good queen who had learnt from her sister that LOVE was the key to controlling her powers.

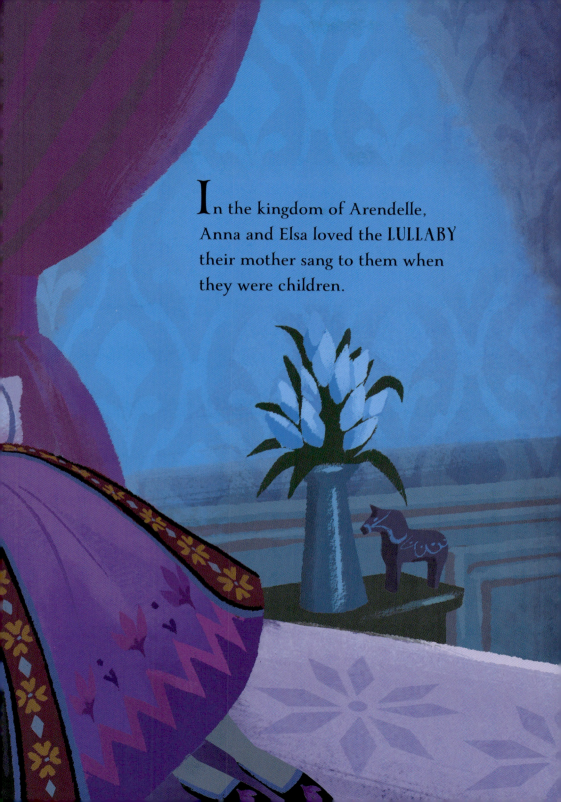

In the kingdom of Arendelle, Anna and Elsa loved the LULLABY their mother sang to them when they were children.

The lullaby was about a SECRET RIVER,
which held all the answers about the past.
It gave the girls a lot to think about and
excited their IMAGINATIONS.

As time went on, Anna and Elsa grew older. Elsa discovered her magical power over SNOW AND ICE, which became stronger and stronger. One night, a MYSTERIOUS VOICE called to her. What did it want?

Elsa realised that the
voice wanted her to travel
north. She went to the fjord
and shot out an enormous

ICY BLAST!

It was clear that Elsa's magic had done something new and powerful. BUT WHAT DID IT MEAN?

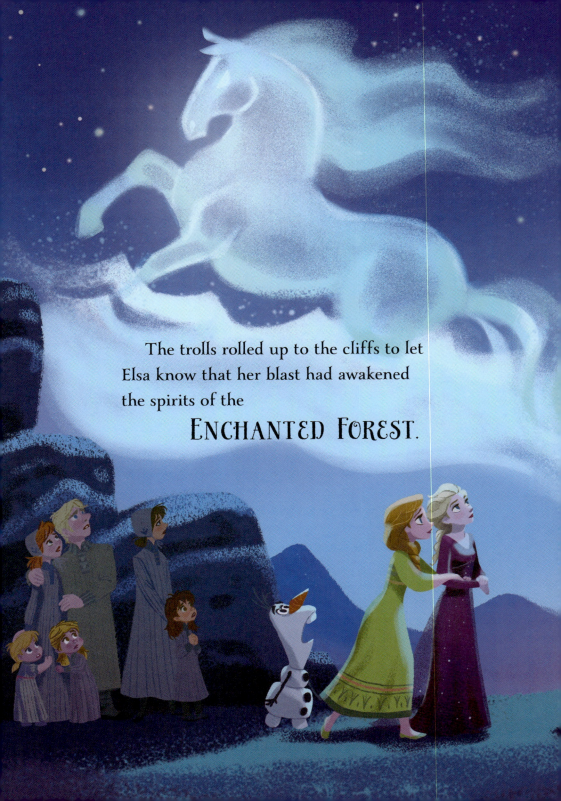

The trolls rolled up to the cliffs to let Elsa know that her blast had awakened the spirits of the

ENCHANTED FOREST.

They warned her that the spirits were
ANGRY. The forest was also where a nomadic
group of people called the NORTHULDRA
were said to live.

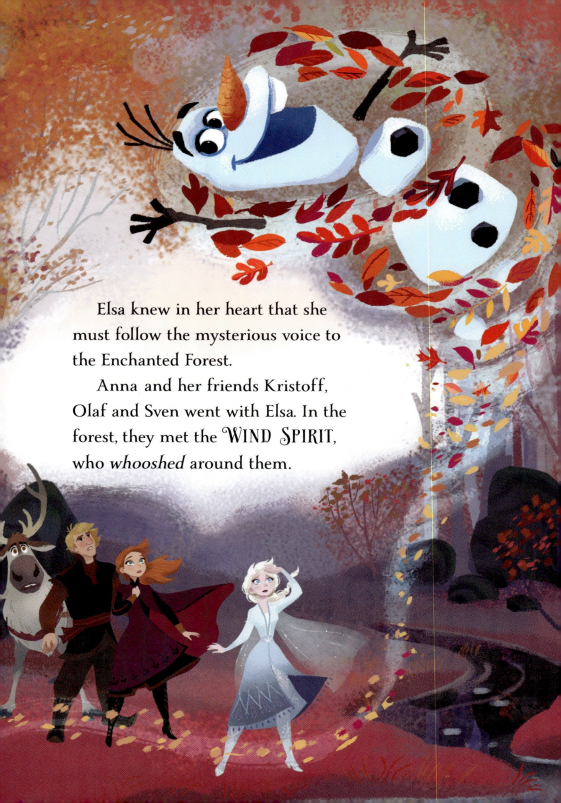

Elsa knew in her heart that she must follow the mysterious voice to the Enchanted Forest.

Anna and her friends Kristoff, Olaf and Sven went with Elsa. In the forest, they met the WIND SPIRIT, who *whooshed* around them.

They also met the Northuldra people, who told them STORIES and revealed that they were more SIMILAR to Elsa, Anna and their friends than they were DIFFERENT.

While Elsa and her friends were
getting to know the Northuldra,
the mighty FIRE SPIRIT appeared
and set the Enchanted Forest on fire!
Elsa tried to STOP the spreading fire
with her magic, but it wasn't working.

Kristoff HELPED Anna and the
reindeer escape the flames.

Elsa was finally able to calm
the Fire Spirit by feeding it
SNOWFLAKES. The Fire Spirit
was actually a little salamander.
Elsa heard the voice again,
and she noticed that the
Fire Spirit could hear it, too.

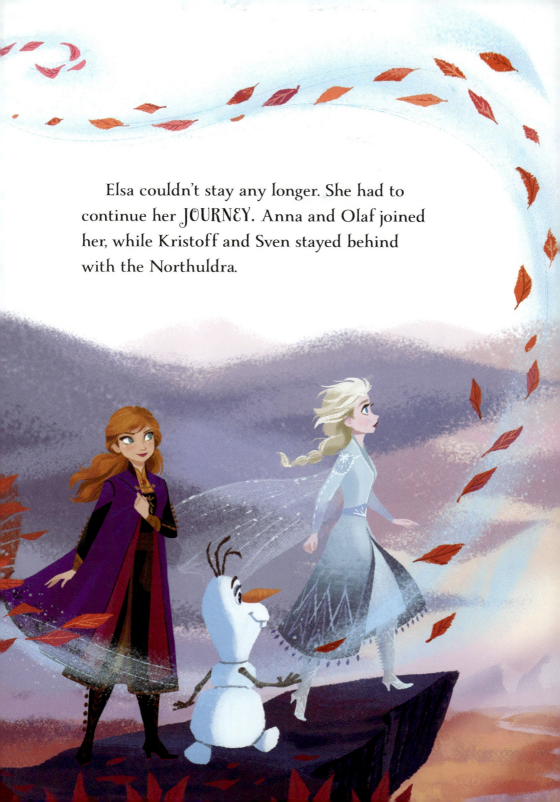

Elsa couldn't stay any longer. She had to continue her JOURNEY. Anna and Olaf joined her, while Kristoff and Sven stayed behind with the Northuldra.

Heading north, Anna and Elsa discovered
their PARENTS' SHIPWRECK!

Inside the ship, they studied a map and
learnt that their parents had travelled north
to understand why Elsa had magic.

Elsa feared losing Anna, just as she had
lost their parents. Elsa decided to make the
rest of the journey alone.

With a heavy heart, Elsa formed a boat made of ice that SCOOPED UP Anna and Olaf and carried **them safely away**.

Anna and Olaf couldn't stop the boat after Anna accidentally steered it towards the sleeping EARTH GIANTS. Anna and Olaf kept quiet as they passed them.

More determined than ever, Elsa reached
the next part of her journey: the DARK SEA.
Now she needed to cross it.

The WATER NOKK reared up from the
sea and tried to stop Elsa. After a fierce battle,
Elsa and the Water Nokk realised that their
powers were equal. A mutual respect formed
between them.

Meanwhile, Anna and Olaf's journey continued into a cave, where an ICE SCULPTURE appeared in front of them. It was a signal from Elsa. The journey had answered some of the queen's questions.

Elsa had FINALLY ARRIVED in the north!
The voice that had called to her now quietened
to a WHISPER, and she realised it had been within
her all along. It had guided her to discover her
inner peace.

By working together, the sisters were able to
restore peace and harmony to the land at last.